The Giving of Pears

Black Lawrence Press
www.blacklawrence.com

Executive Editor: Diane Goettel
Book Design: Steven Seighman

Black Lawrence Press
115 Center Ave
Aspinwall, PA 15215
U.S.A.

Published 2010 by Black Lawrence Press, an imprint of Dzanc Books

Cover painting: *Pirum*, by Jeff Faust

ISBN: 978-0-9826364-3-5

First edition 2010

Printed in the United States

The Giving of Pears

poems
by

Abayomi Animashaun

Black Lawrence Press
New York

Dear Rita,
it was really
nice meeting you
at the Gist
Street Reading.
I wish you immense
joy and happiness
— abayo

Table of Contents

Going to School

Lagos

Sunday Mornings at the Barber Shop

The Unseen

The Other Testament

The Tailor and His Strings

for

Rachel Ray:

Who initiated me into the mysteries

& stayed till I understood the signs

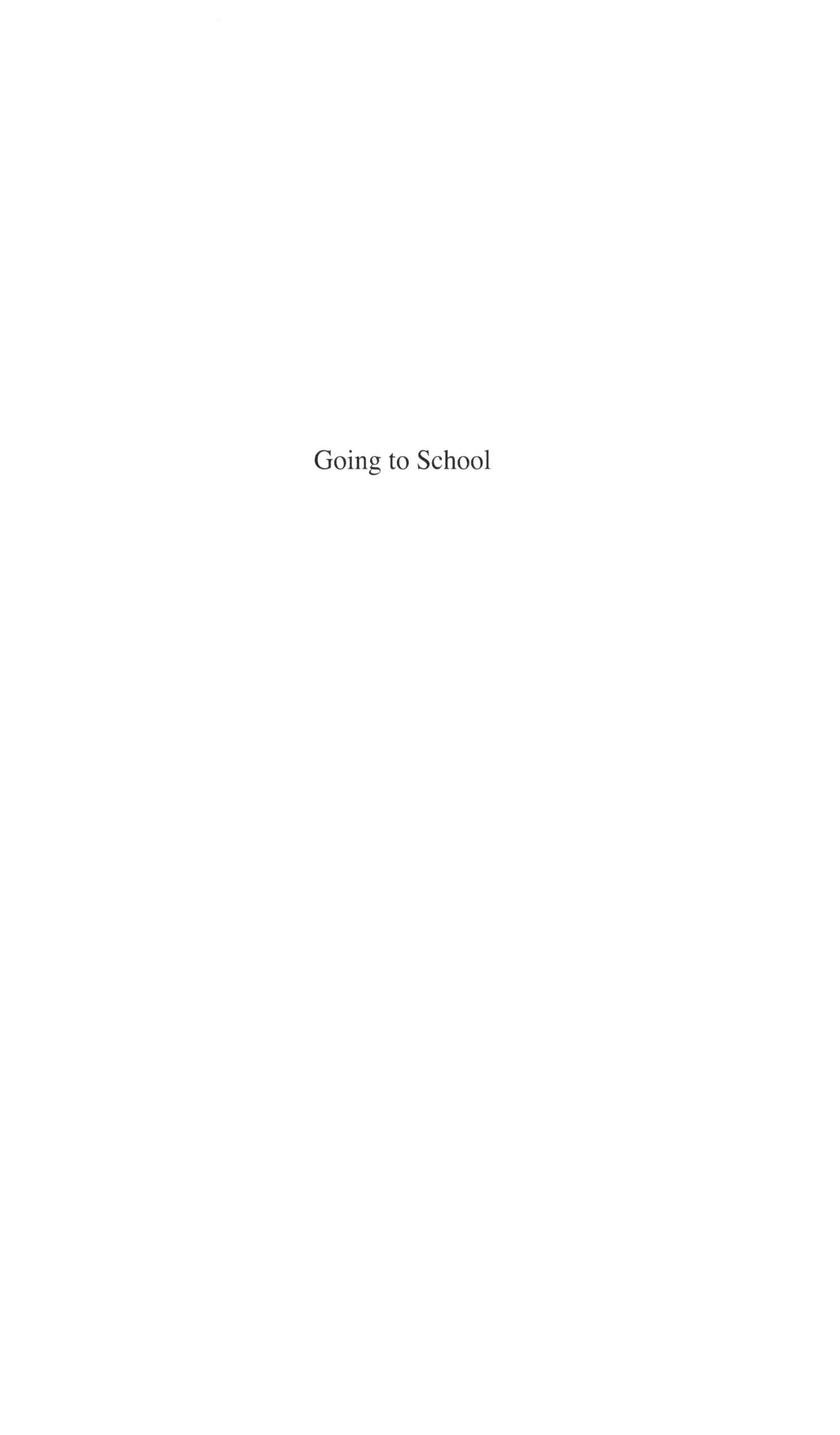

Going to School

Going to School

The robes are washed. The sandals are ready.
I am finally going to that school within myself.
The prophets say the principal is beautiful and
Walks around naked. The teachers are drunks
Who eat from the same bowls as antelopes and
Invite old fish to tea. I am most excited about the
Scientists who, if it is true, spend day and night
In long dim corridors looking through telescopes
Furiously taking notes. They've been in here
Without food for years. Rumor has it days ago
One of them, gaunt and ecstatic, ran out raving
How he'd found happiness within the moon's
Black spots and how he can mend the sun's sad
Yellow by wiping the blisters on stones along a river
And placing them gently within the sun's dull light.
An old fish, thin and trembling, is here as guide.
We sit on the mat, drink tea, share stories.
Tomorrow, the first lessons begin.

Temple of Edible Fruits

Just as it is possible to enter the temple
Of the unutterable through the colors
Of Cezanne, so it is with holding
An unpeeled orange to the sun,
Rotating it gently in the light,
Until a window, dark and magnificent,
Reveals itself on your purple wall:
Inside, the apple with its green
Mustache and red tie is giving
A sermon and has just said: 'Sun
Speak our prayer': In front, a young
Altar peach is holding the cross
Of a dead fish. The pear-usher walks
Into the aisle and raises the collection-basket
To the old pineapple wiping her son's nose.
She reaches into her purse, slowly pulls out
A coin, engraved with a man rotating
An orange to the sun's light.

Tomato

Before slicing
And throwing it on a pan
Pay attention,
And if you have the eye
You'll find, on its side,
A wooden door with a brass handle.
Push slowly, and enter
A village with its own silent physics.
Its own reddened curvature:
Yellow is the face of the newborn.
Green, the tired hat of the old.
Here sand is red,
And goats lead their shepherd
Through a narrow yard's edge.
Doves wash their breasts
At the mouth of a black river.
Children with white seeds on their heads
Tie gray wet clouds on their waists,
Leap around in a circle and sing of light.
Of soil. Of their readiness to be plucked
And wiped by a calloused hand.

Kettle

Pour in some water.
Set it on a lit stove.
Listen:

Inside the contraption
Is a village where pregnant women
Gather round guava trees

To barter the shapes and colors
Of their unborn.

They have gathered round
Another guava tree.

In your kitchen,
The kettle lurches.

One woman, tall and round in the face begins:

“I want mine short. With yellow feet and rigid joints.
It matters little if it’s a girl or boy.”

The other women agree.

The kettle lurches.

She gives birth.

In the kitchen,
We hear the first whistle.

Another, lean with sinewy legs adds:

"I want both together. One part boy.
One part girl. One side orange. The other side blue."

The women agree. She gives birth.

The kettle lurches,
The whistling intensifies.

The pace picks up.

One wants a full grown woman
With the head of a hyena.

Another, an infant with full beard,
Holding a knife.

The next, a tree with colorless branches
And brown leaves.

The one after, a lizard with boys' legs
Completely drunk on palm wine.

On and on, until...

The kettle rages.
Whistles maniacally,

And lets out the white breath
Of the tired women birthing at the village square.

Antecdote of a Goat

There, is one with slackened tie.
Beside him an old paper and a black umbrella.

He is dreaming of his lost love:

A goat with no horns, hooves, and hide.
With the voice of a saddened woman
Her head buried in the wet corners of her blouse.

She is dreaming of a man with horns, hooves, and hides.
Beside him an old paper and an umbrella.

His neck-tie slackened, he too is lost in a dream.

One he'll soon forget: of a man dreaming himself
Loving a goat desperate for a woman dreaming the man.

Ballad of the Drunk

I fell in love with a tree once. Swaying she
Giggled as I touched her,
Pulled down her branches and
Wiped sweat from her brow.

My! She was bleached white
With purple ears and burgundy eyes.

A fantastic tree.
Always naked. Unvined.
Gloriously transparent
In the wind's white arm.

Oh! To hear her laugh…

See how she stands:
Robeless among the grass:

…Just to be naked beside her.
To lay hold and dance beside her.

(No, I haven't had too much to drink.
No man can ever have too much to drink.)

…Just to give her from this gourd
And lead her past the shadows at my door.

Lagos

Lagos

Old city.

Daily, I hear such
Horrible news about you:

An infant burnt
And sold for parts.

Priests knowing
Other men's wives.

Boys, hired as killers:

Beautiful city:

Body of island
Beside the lagoon.

Face of a woman
Sweeping the grave
Of her husband.

Voices of masquerades
Dancing on black-tarred streets:

Don't turn your back on us.

Is it the priest
Casting false oracles?

Is it the governor
Stealing from people?

Or are there too many of us
No room is left you to breathe?

Home of nicely sown
Sokoto and buba.

Home of freshly cooked
Moi-moi and eko:

Lead us into that pure elegance.
The one the ancients knew,
When the oracle first revealed:

..this shall be among the most loved
Of all the cities in the world...

History Lesson

On the wall is a map of places the so-called explorers
— Mungo Park and the rest of them —
Discovered. But did they know
Of my longing to kiss you tonight?

Did those leaders who went to Berlin
In 1885, when they sought to open a 'dark continent',
Did they know of my need to ravage your breasts
Holding you against the cold stove?

(This is taking too long!) Why not travel to my chest,
And I to yours on that bed
You know so well, and rewrite history
The way we know how?

Love Poem

How I've been told to leave love poems
With Dulcinea and Don Quixote.
And if tragic, Hamlet and Ophelia.
How then to express this turn of my soul
At you spread so innocently upon the mat
With angels plaiting into your hair
The precise constellation of the big dipper
And pulling the slender rope of your feet,
Setting off the measured bells of your heart.
How to reenter your moan and how
To pencil the ineffable centered therein.
Always I come away with tailored meanings:
In there must be a Rapunzel reddening
In countenance beside an apple, letting loose,
A second time, her hair along the castle wall.
A Moses kissing the breasts of a Zeporrah
Away from the sheep in a tent on Sinai.
Or a Snow White finally guiding the mouth
Of a dwarf right before she comes:
But how right they are, those poets.
I have no words in the machinery of my soul
For how you've just pulled me to you.
Released my belt and, now, steadying me
Across the blue flood into the new country.

At a Supermarket

At a supermarket an old man in white shirt,
Tucked in blue jeans, sees my hand in yours
And shakes his head in disapproval.

We pick eggs, bread, doughnuts.
You raise your nose as we walk past
The meat cooler with cow-tongues and ox-tails.

In the beverage aisle, two women look at you
As if you stole something from them.
They roll their eyes at me. You don't notice. I do.

First check lanes, then doors, where the old man still stands
– In disapproval. My hand finds yours. I call you pale one.
You call me monkey.

Way of the Moon

In this city the moon
Walks the streets
Dressed in white damask

Have you seen her

Out there in your garden
Filled with guavas
She is taking a bath

Even darkness gathers
Around her white dress
Hung loose by the well

Leaving Lagos

— After Cavafy

As you set out to leave Lagos
Wish that the way be long
Full of adventure, full of knowledge.

Wish that the way be long
And for mornings filled with such joy
As when you enter the ports the first time.

Always keep Lagos in your mind.
But, do not hurry the journey.
Better if it lasts many years.

If now you find her poor, Lagos
Did not betray you. Without her
You would not have set out at all.

And if you find yourself in that country an old man
Remember, Lagos gave you the beautiful journey.
She has no more to give you.

By then, with all your wisdom, all your experience
And rich with all you would have gained along the way
You will understand what Lagos means.

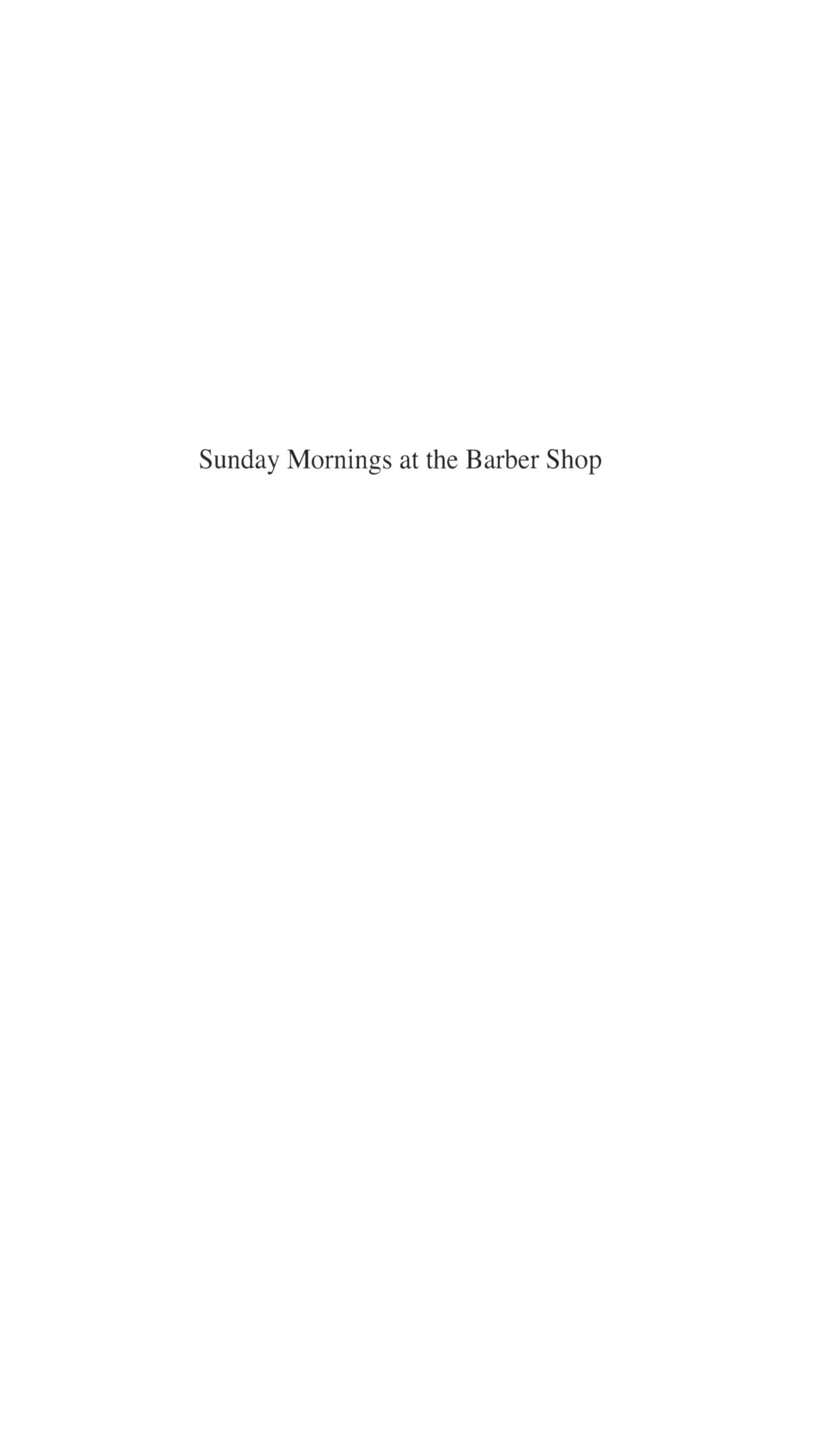

Sunday Mornings at the Barber Shop

Sunday Mornings at the Barber Shop

On Sunday mornings
When services begin,
The angels hang their wings,
Abandon their temples,

And come down for a haircut
And nice shave.

The barber, now bent
And squinting with age,

Never says: ‘Why,
On Sunday mornings,

This long row of men
Waiting patiently
In dazzling white suits?’

Only, ‘next’, or
‘How would you like it?’

‘Next,’ and Lucifer
Steps up.

The barber,
Rubs his face and head
Hard with water and sea-salt,

Until the bruise and soot
Begin to disappear,

And the burnt and gummed-down
Hair, emerge.

The barber looks up momentarily,

Next is one now reading
On the latest fashion.

He shrugs his shoulders
And sets to work on Lucifer:

Who is holding a map of a village, where
Tomorrow, volcanoes will erupt.

Marriage of Demons

The Ceremonies begin
The moment you sleep.

Then, one after the other,
The Leaves, Vines,
Broken Tree Trunks, emerge.

These are the dignitaries.

Witnesses arrive soon after:

Children drowned at sea.
Elders living beyond death.

Even the child who for years
Died when you felt
You'd given birth,

Even she is there
With your round face,
Your wife's eyes,
The high-cheekbone
Of your great grand-father.

And there are others
Belonging to people
You know and don't:

After them,
The bride comes
Gossamer in the Moon's
Stretched gown,

And the groom, pallid
In Death's gray suit.

Through the night,
They beat their drums loud,
Paying you no mind.

The ceremonies end
The moment you awake.

The Giving of Pears

Give an infant a pear,
And all the iguanas in the village
Gather on the bank of the old river
And lick the stones until they become green.

For angels to descend,
Remove their wings and begin shouting
And playing like children in the old river,
Give a soft ripened one to a widower.

And if you must see the dead:
A husband gutted-clean in a car accident;
A child drowned in the village well:

Invite a maiden to your house.
Give her a cup of water from that old river.
And place in her hands a freshly plucked pear.

Breathing

In the end, it too
Is the story of the prodigal son:

Inhale:

And look
There he is at your door
Broken and in rags

Exhale:

And senseless with joy
You clasp, kiss, embrace

Inhale:

And your other son,
Calloused from working the fields
Seethes in rage

Exhale:

And you wash the feet of the one
Just returned, and bless the other
Saying 'blessings my son, this house is yours'

Inhale:

And the seething continues

Exhale:

And the one newly returned,
Repentant, sets to work about the house

Inhale:

And the other takes what's his and leaves:

Now you must learn to be breathless again
For moments at a time

When the one goes for firewood
Or sets about town for his brother.

He is in town again, and lost.
This time he won't return.

And you remain seated.
Lifeless by the window.
Your eyes closed.

Miracles

It is okay that we do not know how
Much of it happens. That an infant, lost
In the forest and feared taken by spirits,
Can emerge years later seeking her parents.
That an old man with a cane barely moving
His feet from fatigue can raise both hands,
With the enemy near, ready to impress,
And part the sea. Or that a widow
Can become whole after months
Of lining the street with her blood,
Simply by touching the mud-soiled garment
Of one oblivious to her ailment.
It is enough to know that faith is a necessary
First step. And, in most cases, the only step.
The ridiculous aside: jumping off the ledge,
Hoping for a sweeping catch by the angel Gabriel:
But knowing also that when broken and lost,
Uriel too can wear the face of a child, run
In front of us, utter nonsense, and make us laugh.
And that Michael, impatient with my sad heart,
Can lead this orange seller again to my house.

Waiting

So what if doves you thought
Had flown away with autumn
Return to your hut and gather again
Outside your door?

So what if Orpheus, armed with songs,
Descended into the underworld
And nearly returned with the woman
He loved and lost?

Myth is myth.

But only less so if each dove,
Returned, is a reincarnation
Of a love back from the underworld.

Only less so, if after its cooing
The dove turned into the woman
You lost: who, you imagine,
Is leaning by the kitchen window

Holding both hands to her chest, saying:
Orpheus led; my love followed:

Right now, a dove is at your door.
This isn't a dream anymore.
Get up. Straighten your hair.
Rinse those grapes on the table.

Oh! What news she has.
What gossip from the underworld.

How to Speak the Language of Birds

It is not as hard
As it sounds.

Three steps really.

First:

You need only wait
For the flock to arrive.

How you wait:

On one foot,
Your neck crooked:

Does not matter.

Where you wait:

A garden, park,
Or junkyard:

This too,
Does not matter.

Be sure to have bread crumbs
At the ready.

Seeing you
With its morning meal, one

Wayward among them
Will alert the rest to your kindness.

Don't be afraid when they flap
And inch toward you.

Second:

Pay attention to how they,

On this morning,
Bend their necks and peck
At the scattered pieces.

Bend and peck
At the scattered pieces also.

After all,
This is a communion.

Last:

On the third day,
One among the flock
Will meet and lead you into the fold.

Tear and sprinkle the loaves again.
Only, this time, listen

To the pecking and cooing,
Fluttering and crooking.

Do likewise.

There will be no visions.
No trances.
No spells of delirium.

Arrive early
The following day,

And watch
As the miracle of that morning
Begins to unfold.

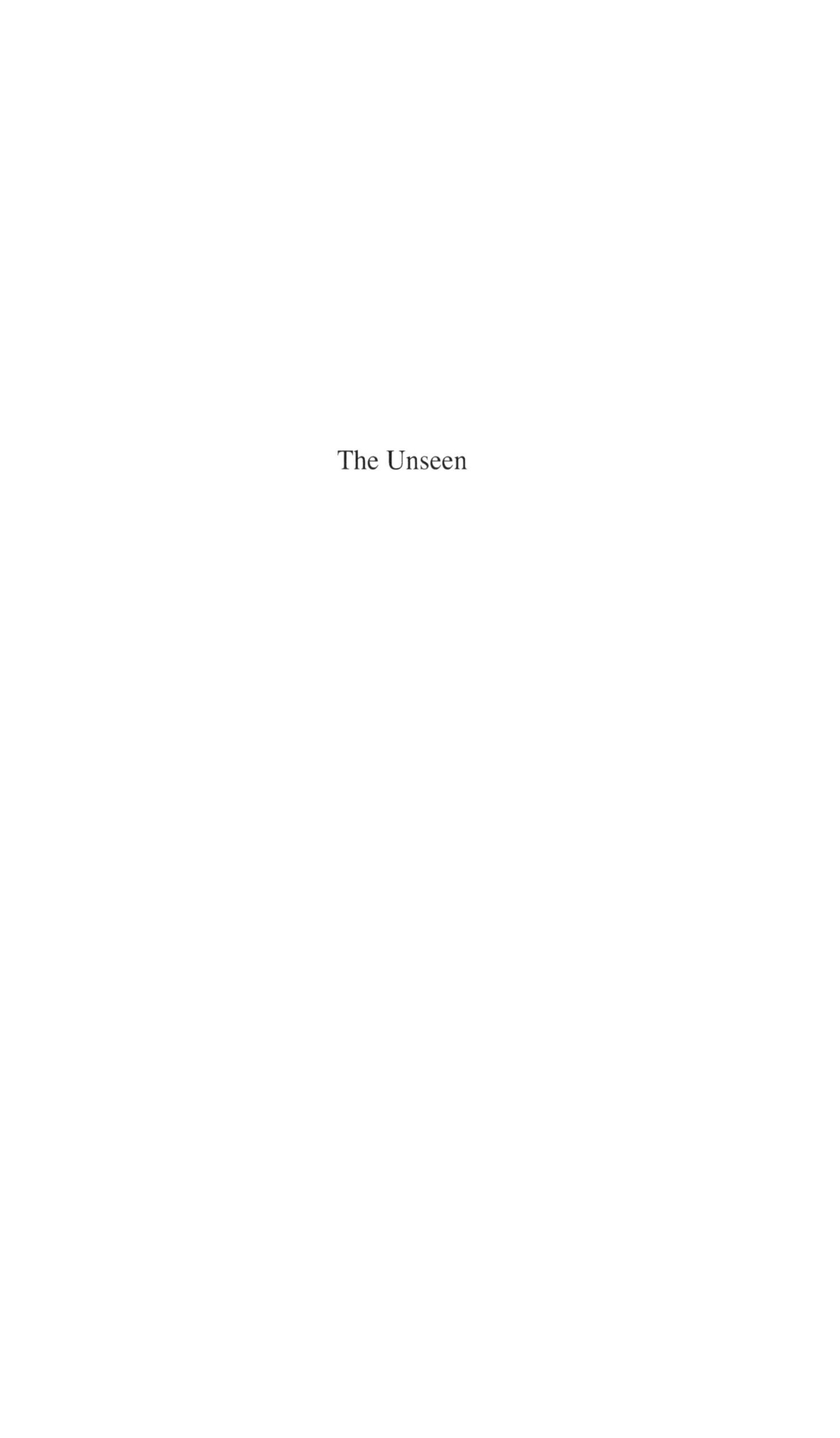

The Unseen

The Unseen

They come with the second flood:
At the hour when
We are wound in the dullness
Of our daily work:

Singing the tunes before the first words,
Before the separation,
Before the creator got drunk on wine
And left the act to the hen.

They come carrying
Trays with no trinkets,
Their cold bodies gleaming dark
From rivers with no water.

–

On the streets, we don't see
The long rounded shapes
Of their footprints, nor
Hear their murmurings.

Still, everyday and in the same hour,
They sit beside us. Wash their infants
Beside us and conduct their festivals.

They send their children to their school
To learn their own alphabets and
Make their own music.

–

We await their dark arrival:
That gust of wind,

That last minute breath
Against the thatched leaves.

The fire catches:

The carpenter tightens his grip,
Pounds in place that nail with the hammer.
The farmer pulls hard at the weeds.
The school teacher, again, points a stick
At the map of a people near-forgotten.
The student raises her head from a book.
The man, locked-gentle with another woman,
Feels the sudden need to be home.

My Son

The boy I never had
Goes to school
Somewhere.
Every morning,
He packs his bag
And walks away
From the other
Boys and girls.

He skips school a lot
Distracted on his way
By rats, lizards,
And spectator cats on window sills.
Sometimes,
While chasing a stray,
He winds up at the school gates
And goes in grudgingly...

He sleeps during lectures,
Questioning the need
For adding or subtracting
Using such stupid tools
As numbers.
Nothing in school matters,

Save the stories
Of occupations and conquests,
Rebellions and uprisings.
He sleeps during
And after recess.
Most times, he is asleep
When the final bell rings.

After school,
He returns
To the village of the unborn
To join the other children,
Everyday wondering
About the uselessness of school
And the fool who denies him life.

Loss

Such lies have been told about her.
My favorite: 'when she comes
The blue hand of the sky vanishes.
Hippos storm the sun.
Birds peck furiously at anthills.
Winds wrap tightly against trees.'
But notice how she doesn't say a word
And sits beside you when
The moments of love have flickered their last.
How she stands beside you when solitude
Has you cornered. Right now she is outside
Rinsing her hair. Later, she'll use it
To wipe the mirrors of your heart.

Son of Orpheus

He comes from the village
Where much is reversed:

Infants fetching water.
The old having a boxing match.

Dogs pounding yam.
Doves washing clothes:

He doesn't wear a musician's robe
As most would expect.

Nor carry the wooden flute
Or lyre of his father.

He goes to the bar
Tips the waitress generously

Then raises his cup to her.
Sitting beside him,

You hear no music.
Just talk about a wasted cloud

And blue as the color of the heart.
Only after you return

And are alone
Do you hear songs

From the collapsed temple within.
And you break out singing.

Brimming. Happy.

Your neighbors, the ones
Who for years thought you joyless

Will enter your song,
And stay so till dawn.

In the morning, each will say:

Look! The old man
Whose song brings forth dawn.

An Ordinary Day

Nothing special. An ordinary day.
Trees waving on their height.
Squirrels knocking at my door.
Dead friends walking in and out of walls.

The Visit

This morning,

Death brushed its cold fingers
Across my face and, sullen, said:

Your father
Will lose his sight again.

It is not good for the dead
To suffer a second blindness.

And I, cold and shaking
From its presence:

'What will you have me do?'

We can use yours, It said
Or that of your unborn son

And with no second thought
'My unborn son'.

–

In the dark world of the unborn,
My son, playing quietly by the sea,
Forgets the curved mechanism of light
Inside a small fish.

Ancestors

Not many remain in their graves as we would expect of the dead:

Some wander out of their pits, or if buried beneath a sacred stone, burst out of their sepulchers and roam the streets at the dark hours of the early morning.

No rotten corpses here. Or, flesh-eating monsters return from the dead. Just quiet spirits, alive in the belly of the wind, whistling their old songs when it is howling:

At times telling us stories about themselves: Especially, when we've forgotten tales of our birth.

The wind against my window has stiffened: I know my grandfather is in the kitchen sniffing for meat in the pot of soup...

The lid is rattling: He likes the aroma...

Now, the howling is intense: The pot is tittering on the stove...

I go into the kitchen. Remove the meat. Sever it in two. And leave a bowl of cold water beside it.

Suffering

Time to accept *it* as part of the package. Instead of an unwanted stray: A temporary nuisance come to cause a slight disturbance.

Time to accept the woes that befall us as not *goofs* of some god: Locked down with petitions from his believers. Or, as you say 'his precious flock':

Who, sore by week's end from their jobs. Come to clean the synagogue. Not to mention how they give alms to the poor.

There's no use finding it hard to feel. That the one to whom you kneel and beat your heart. Merely sat aside and watched...

As your door got broken into by boys: Who pummeled and set your face on fire. Tore into your wife. And left her mangled and near dead on the ground.

Time to start believing that this god, is a god of indiscriminate ways: That *evil* is a deed destined not only for the wicked.

That, he is a god who blesses us all alike. And, when bored, is willing to wager us all like cowries.

This same god: To whom you insist on raising your heart in faith. To deliver your wife from this agony. And both of you, this pain.

A New Religion

It sounds pompous. And, at best, done:

Each claiming a new way. Each with its leader standing behind a lectern raising his hands. Blessing those present...

And they with eyes closed listening intently to rhythms, say, of the holy ghost. Or, for our purposes. Its equivalent.

But imagine. And stay with me on this. One where everyone already belonged: Those dead as well. And still to come.

Temples made of strands from each person's breath. Candles lit with dreams of the dead.

Rituals performed in the language of the unborn. And hymns, the movement of bodies stretching alone in bed. Or, beside a loved one.

And imagine each man being his own *Good News*: A ready-made priest able to minister quietly to the needs of his own heart. When all departs.

That the homeless under the bridge. With the mucous. And cold sneeze. Contributes to the day's hymn.

And the man, who last year broke my heart, is now arriving at his new lover's house. A priest, I hope, of loving heart. Waiting for him in the bedroom. Nude. Ready to share of his own good news.

The Other Testament

The Other Testament

In the other testament, god, bored from the predictable songs of angels, put his godly attributes aside and became human...

In the first book, he tried his hand at fishing. And, new to rowing, suffered from a sense of direction. Dizzy, he was stranded at sea for days. Only to be rescued by fishermen from the other village.

In the second book, he decided to be a shepherd since this was the profession of many of his prophets. But running after a sheep before it falls into a ditch, guiding the herd to the right field, even when all seems bleak, reminded him too much of his old status.

In the third, he was a carpenter. But so used to looking down, suffered from a severe case of vertigo when climbing a ladder. Three times he fell off a building and broke his wrists.

In the fourth, he worked for a butcher but was soon fired for being too kind to dogs. Then, he tried his hand at wrestling, only to suffer defeat after humiliating defeat. All took turns throwing him and pinning his back to the ground. Even the village bard, who couldn't throw a child, scored a victory against him in no time.

In the final book, god decided to be a farmer. Only, at harvest, he came short of the right amount of cassava. Even the cocoa yams that he was so proud of perished from locusts.

In the last paragraph of the other testament, god, thin from hunger, weary from effort, and dreading the money lender's wrath, wept hard in the corner of his house. And, ashamed, cried for Gabriel and the other angels to guide him back to his place...

The Good Samaritan

It is an interesting adjective, the word *good*, placed by a man who many know simply by the name of his town. Mostly forgetting that he could have been born of a carpenter. Or, if the reputation of his town is to hold, a thief, a high-ranking member of the bandits that terrorized the neighboring cities.

Yet, we call him good... From one act... How lucky for him that we'll never know whether he peeked through the cracks of the bathroom to watch the priest's daughter bathing. He, a man near sixty. She, a girl barely sixteen. No way for us to know of the burning he suffered and how he followed the girl from afar hoping for moments alone with her.

Still, we call him good. Because, coming home again from the tavern. Drunk as he often is. Thinking of the girl. His pants wet with semen. He finds a man lost on the road. Badly bruised. Almost without breath. Left for dead...

And what does it matter if the only reason he carried the young man to the inn. Paid for the keeper to wash, feed, and clothe him was simply because he thought he was the girl's older brother returning from Tyre. The one he had heard her talk so often about. The one who rejected the priesthood and followed a caravan as far as the Sahara.

...What does it matter. Good is *good*. Even though that night, after paying the inn-keeper, he hurried back to his town. Climbed and sat atop a tree not far from the girl's house and dreamed her naked. Her thighs wet. Their moans gentle. Both shaking. Trying to hold each other steady through those hours before dawn.

Noah

The first afternoon we met, he talked about the flood. I told him about the goats in the barn. How sick they were and unable to move. He talked about god being tired and sick of how little we cared for Him. The immenseness of the water coming. And the doves, goats, and sheep he'd gathered already. I tried listening. He left that day unhappy he couldn't get through to me.

The next time he came, his cheeks had tightened. His face was long. His eyes deep. He talked as is if I wasn't there. 'The ark is almost complete' he said. 'Even the tiniest animals have been captured'. He said I had ten days to make up my mind. He left before I could tell him. My sick goats had died, and I was avoiding the money lender.

He called again. The night before the tenth day. He was drenched. Shaking, and sneezing hard. I asked him to sit. Made tea. Measured honey with dried flour. Tired. Empty. He said 'prostitutes spit in my face. They douse me with water and drag me on the ground'. Then he said, 'come into the ark'. I told him I couldn't leave my goats. 'They are finally gaining weight. Tomorrow,' I said 'I'll be selling my first one in a long time to the carpenter across the river.' We remained silent for a while. He finished his tea. Thanked me and left.

On the tenth day, I waited to see if the rain would fall like he said. Nothing. I sold the goat. Waited. The eleventh day. Sold a goat to the village smith. Paid the money lender. Waited. The twentieth day. Nothing. Walking back from selling another to the butcher. I see Noah in a collapsed boat outside his house, fitting a dry leaf into a dove's mouth.

Fragments from 'The Lost Memoir of Enoch'

I

...Unlike prophets who after birth called their mothers by name. Or had frequent visits from angels at a young age. I, at best, was deficient. Utterly mediocre...

III

...Worse than the decrepit sheep of the family, I was more...the vermin. Worthy of stone practice from children shooting slings.

IV

My father would have allowed it. How often he regretted my birth when his best friends spoke of Ishmael. Who wrestled a goat to the ground. And no doubt will be a mighty hunter.

V

Or Isaac, who swam a mile before rescuing a sheep drowning in the river. But, being a barber never sat well with my father. And I can still see him throwing up his arms. Shouting 'you'll only waste time polishing other people's mustaches with a knife'...

IX

The only time he left me with his hen, I fell asleep beside it from the day's heat. And woke up to find it stolen. How he cursed my mother loudly for giving birth to a nit, who...

XX

It is no mystery I became a prophet. But imagine my father's doubt when the old men of our town arrived with the news and saying blessings to our house.

XXI

Or how speechless he was when his dying mother forced herself from bed. Knelt at my feet and prayed 'holy one, please ask god to forgive my sins'...

XXIII

And how years later, on his bed. He tried raising his head to ask forgiveness not from god. But his 'vermin of a son'. 'The failed polisher of moustaches'. Who didn't die in his mother's womb. And is not yawning behind the old priests...

XXIV

...But is standing in front. Saying all the prayers he knows to the god who chose him and now calls his father home.

The Night Mohammed Came

He entered my hut muttering to himself. He had been traveling a long time in the desert. And was hungry. His robe was filthy. His feet caked in mud. He looked gaunt. Desperate. Ready to devour the mouse burrowing its way out the door. I asked about his journey. What village he visited and where he might be going. He kept muttering. About food. Apples, especially. And grapes.

Later, after I had washed his feet and removed his robe. After the bread and wine. We sat in the dim glow of a lighted candle and talked into the night. He talked about Moses being the father of false prophets. 'The old liar' he said yawning, 'claiming there is only one god'. He finished his wine. And, slightly drunk started talking about the Greek goddess Athena. How he'd like to take her to dinner and have a drink or two with her. Maybe even get her drunk to see if she'd lose her helmet. Hop on the table and dance around naked.

I talked about the virtues of polygamy. How I desire the girl who sells oranges. 'My wife is old' I said, 'if only I had enough sheep to pay the girl's dowry'. But he was already snoring loudly on the mat. I blew out the candle and made for the door. Only to hear him speak in his sleep. 'Leave the light on. And you should know, Gabriel and a few other angels are in the next village gathered at the mouth of your girlfriend's window watching her undress.'

Potiphar's Wife

When the story is told, they'll say: I stole into a room with a boy. Pushed him onto the chair. And, loosened my dress.

And they'll say: when the poor boy refused, I fearing shame. Being a bitch. Sent my stupid Potiphar after him.

I don't deny whoring myself to a young man. But listen to my side: Potiphar himself sought the boy. And dreamed himself naked beside him. He spoke often of Joseph's ripped arms. Muscled thighs. And broad back.

And how, he fantasized about the organ between the boy's thighs.

Not once did he touch me. Much less throw himself at me. Burning. Impassioned. Recklessly absorbed.

And when he fantasized, I followed along. Down the boys lips. My tongue on his well-hewned neck. Biting and stroking his back. Before putting my mouth gently on his organ.

To feel like a woman... Married to a powerful man who loves boys. You are left biting your tongue. And when the bastard is drunk. He'll even invite you to watch.

Imagine how lit up I was when alone with the boy. And he asked what was wrong. How bitterly I complained. How much I confessed...

He understood. Then, he untied his robes. He was loosening mine. When the *fucking* eunuch arrived. How to explain the nakedness. The girth. The inflamed breasts.

So I acted. Said: *he forced his way into my house. But I resisted.* The truth would have been worse. And our necks would have known it.

I was the one, who acting violated, sowed the idea in my husband of throwing him in the cell. Among the vagabond others. Then praying with all my heart the boy finds a way out.

As for my husband. He's found another child. Built and well proportioned like Joseph. While I remain *a wife*. Locked up in my house. Guarded by eunuchs and female servants.

David

When word came
That he thrust his sword
Into a man's throat,
Those present sighed:
Kill that son of a Donkey!

The Town's folk
Had grown so used to him
Playing 'Conqueror & Slave',
'Divinely Chosen
& Destined for Defeat'.

A few months ago,
He was wielding a sword
And shouting:
Gather the women of the city.
Send them into the sinners' midst.

Our spies confirm, their champion
Lifts two men with one hand
And downs a barrel of wine with the other.

Before the word came,
No one had seen him for weeks.

The old shepherd who brought the news
Said: *he's in the mountain, naked,*
Armed with a sword and catapult,
Raving about letting fly a stone,
Rocking a giant to the ground,

And stabbing him complete.
The old man, his head now buried
And sobbing uncontrollably, continued:
The man he murdered was no man at all,
But my boy of eleven, just learning to tend sheep.

The Burning Bush

It should matter little
That no burning occurred

That the dull light glowing
From the gaunt leaves,

Was no invention of a god tired
Of old metaphors

And pointing a tired shepherd
Through a new rite.

It is enough that the light
Was nothing more

Than a pale reflection
Of the prophet's own heart

Renewing itself
And reminding him:

Death brings fresh blessings.
Even in the desert, we are not alone:

It is no wonder Moses removed
His sandals

And prostrated long
As if communing with god.

Though he knew, clear
As that light he swore he saw,

All of it was made up,
And he was just fooling himself.

The Tailor and His Strings

The Tailor and His Strings

There is a village where old men tie strings
Around their chests to hear music from youth:
The ones they hopped to when their legs
Had strength and their hearts were reckless:
Older now and quiet, they go to the tailor,
Himself shaking and old, who measures
The diameter of each weakened heart,
And cuts the string to the appropriate length.
And tightened around each chest, the trembling
Lessens, the shaking fades, and the old man,
Who yesterday could not even speak from grief,
Is now out in the market square buying oranges.

The Sudden Alignment of Mangoes

It is the case that when a mango falls off a table
Without being touched, rolls by itself for days
And reaches the shed of a dog in another village:
Who no doubt will nibble at it till there's no juice left:

It is the case that at the precise moment that fruit
Positions itself behind another waiting to be devoured,
A drunk in a nearby village will wake from his stupor
And claim he's heard the call.

'What moment of clarity,' he'll say,
'What clear direction to follow.'
He'll give up the late night banter with friends
And swear 'the next thing is to clean streets.'

It is the case with such a man that neighbors
Will look on in amazement as he begins
Sweeping graves and darkened alleyways
With children following him around,
Jeering and laughing hard.

And it should come as no surprise
The news will reach his mother:
Who no doubt will entreat, scold,
And remind him of responsibilities.

And when alone, such a man will weep
Steadily in the dark saying:
'How to make do; how to survive...'.

And so it is that at the moment he decides
'To stop the madness', another mango will roll
Precisely behind one waiting to be devoured.

The man will look out his window
And see another, who knew the bottle
Just as hard as he, whistling and raking the gutter.

Listening to Stones With Michelangelo

It is the rock itself that calls.
Its non-voice beckoning at first,

Then echoing so loudly
Your soul, silenced from solitude

And restless for communion,
Reaches for its forehead

And traces its quiet fingers
Across the pimpled eye brows,

The misshapen, slightly raised, nose,
The strong, dented, jaw-line.

But your restless soul won't stop there.
It'll invite the stone into the high

Arching bones of your chest,
Where it resides alone, and excited

It will talk a long time about the Bible
And Greek Mythology:

How Apollo should still be hugging
His beloved tree, Daphne.

How Homer got it wrong,
Polyphemus should be buds with sirens.

How David should also be crucified
And Moses stoned to death:

Only after the stone begins to yawn
Does your soul offer tea laced with gin.

But the stone falls asleep after the first sip,
Starts snoring, and dreaming itself

As a one-eyed woman, humming
And bathing nude beside a river.

If, In My Next Life

If, in my next life, I have a say
In the molding of clay around
My soul, I'd let my heart be sown
With the sun's light and traces
From the blue in Cezanne.
Then, geese would find home
In my hands. Birds seeking
Shelter from storms would
Be unafraid to gather and arrange
Twigs on my skull. And children
Can trail me on my way to work
Picking apples dripping
From my moustache. And
The brave ones can steal behind me
At the bus-stop and pluck guavas
Ripening along the cold black cage
Of my back. And, if billions of years
Later, the light from that heart must
Finally die out, or sixty-seven say,
As it was with Cezanne, it would be
Comforting to know that at least
The universe of my soul would be
Collapsing not into an endless void
As some philosophers have told us,
Or kneeling with some *organless*
Beings singing hymns as reward,
But into its own blue singularity.

Cezanne On Soccer

You must be stubborn,

Willing to stand outside
Till your last sinewed vein

Bulges from sprain
And last element of will

Muscles itself thin.
Keep practicing your drills.

Though it's tempting to
Balance the ball

On your head like this and
Raise it with your foot like that

The ball is best on the ground.
Take each shot like it's your last.

And if you must play with others,
Run around like a mad man.

Leave accuracy to the fancy of those
So conditioned to be *perfect*.

As with painting, your concern
Is with the utmost. Be irreverent:

The moment you have a goalie beaten
Boot that ball into the stands

And watch it transform into a dove,
Mountain, or thousand hands.

And if you are ridiculed,
Kicked off the team,

Return to your drills.
Only then, after many years,

Will the ball reveal itself
And the landscapes within.

Playing Tennis with the Net Down

"...Writing poetry without form is like
playing tennis without a net."
— Robert Frost

I play tennis with the net down,
Rolled across the lawn and pushed
To the side, with sweat heavy on my chest
And the sun glaring on my back.

I practice a slow-paced serve that hangs
In the air long enough for me to travel
To the other side, bring the racquet low
And place another lob high.

All these years friends have pointed
And jeered. *This is no game*, they say.
What purpose to all this?
What point to prove?

Sometimes I watch them go at it.
The tightness on their faces,
The rules waiting to be bent,
All call me back to my ways.

Now children come and watch
The man who plays tennis with his shadow.
They ask if they can stretch the net
Across the lawn,

If they can play fishermen
In long boats on the waters
Ready for a big catch. I nod across at them:
'In this type of tennis, even fishing is possible.'

Rilke's Last Poem

I have become a mirror.

That outside of me is reflected
Fully within. Then, rearranged.

Apples ripened by the sun's light,
Oranges asleep beside the moon,
Guavas whitened among the clouds,

Are here, within my heart.
But the reflections shift and dance.

Clouds seep out of guavas.

Drunk from the sun, apples
Fling their green and red
Dresses to the ground.

And, peeling an orange,
I untie from the moon
A bright yellow scarf.

Acknowledgements

Many thanks to the journals, where these poems first appeared in their early or final forms:

Suffering. The Night Mohammed Came. Son of Orpheus: *5 A.M.* The Unseen. History Lesson. My Son: *Drunken Boat.* Way of the Moon: *Obsidian III.* Playing Tennis with the Net Down: *Southern Indiana Review.* Ancestors: *African American Review.* Leaving Lagos: *New Orphic Review.* Breathing. Waiting: *Oberon.* Anecdote of a Goat. Ballad of the Drunk. Listening to Stones with Michelangelo. Rilke's Last Poem: *Diode.*

Special thanks also to Dave Shumate, Fran Quinn, Caleb Brooks, Allison Wilkins, Lisa Markowitz, Megan Merchant, Heather Jacobs, Kevin Capp, Casey McGrath, Evelyn Gajowski, Aliki Barnstone, and Joseph Dell'Aquila.

ABAYOMI ANIMASHAUN is a Nigerian émigré whose poems have appeared in such journals as *5 A.M.*, *African American Review*, *Drunken Boat*, *Southern Indiana Review*, and *Diode*. A finalist for the Naomi Long Madgett Poetry Prize, Animashaun is a recipient of a grant from the International Center for Writing and Translation.